CANDYFLOSS GUITAR

STEPHEN R. MARRIOTT

Copyright © 2014 Stephen R. Marriott

All rights reserved. No part of this publication may be reproduced, distributed, or transmitted in any form or by any means, including photocopying, recording, or other electronic or mechanical methods, without the prior written permission of the author, except in the case of brief quotations embodied in critical reviews and certain other noncommercial uses permitted by copyright law.

ISBN: 978-1-912145-92-8

To those who have always loved me,
even when my own love was adrift.

CONTENTS

1. Home	11
2. Footsteps	24
3. All Roads Lead Somewhere	46
Acknowledgements	61
About the Author	62

*They are good people who live,
labour, pass by and dream,
and on a day like all the others,
they rest below the earth.*

> – Antonio Machado,
> I Have Walked Down Many Roads

1
HOME

Eduardo opened his wrinkled leather wallet and took out a pile of bank notes. He counted the money twice, put it away and removed a pack of cards from the top pocket of his checkered cotton shirt. Shuffling the cards, he wondered how long it would take for his old comrades to sleep off their hangovers and occupy their usual spots around the table. Occasionally he found himself looking up from the cards and out past his pink candyfloss cart into the sleeping plaza. The sun crept over San Pedro's medieval bell tower and the only signs of life were two backpackers passing through the village, following the route of the ancient pilgrimage of Saint James to Santiago de Compostela, in Spain's north-western limits. Eduardo laughed to himself as he imagined a bunch of tired pilgrims trudging out of town, nursing headaches brought on by cheap wine and the all-night anthems of the brass band and fireworks.

His thoughts were distracted by the arrival of Arnau from inside the bar.

"Eduardo, buen dia. You're setting up shop this morning?" Arnau said with a hint of irony, as he bent down and mopped the plastic table with a wet cloth.

"Yes, it's Sunday, isn't it?" Eduardo said. "But I'm surprised to see you!"

Arnau stood up straight and said, "We Catalan aren't like you Spanish; we work hard and play hard. In Barcelona I'd complete a double shift after spending all night out on the town."

"Please don't patronise me, Arnau, it's my generation that preserved the ideals of work, fought a war for a better Spain. But I'm not sure what for. For people like you to insult our land and for people like my good-for-nothing son to stay in bed all day. In Franco's day the youth had more respect."

"Come on, give us a break," Arnau said as he swiped at a wasp with his cloth, "Diego's not the only one asleep and it is the day after the one and only fiesta this place has to offer! Didn't you fight against the fascists?"

Eduardo turned his head to his candyfloss cart and squinted as he tried to focus on a group of long-legged birds picking their way through the remains of discarded cartons of food at the far side of the plaza. Then he removed a crisp white handkerchief from his trousers, wiped the trenches forming on his brow and said, "Just get me a drink."

"Your usual?"

"Of course! And don't hold back on the rum."

∽

SIPPING HIS CARAJILLO, Eduardo winced as the cheap rum fought with the coffee. He watched the shadows shortening across the plaza as the 'sinners' filed into church with their children behind them. He remembered past fiestas of San Pedro, when the wide-eyed children had queued across the full length of the plaza, pesetas in hand, desperate to taste the clouds of sweet candy. And for a brief moment he smiled as he thought of an earnest Diego spinning the cotton candy onto a stick and his beloved Anna Maria also assisting, stuffing the cotton candy into bags, and collecting the money in the open pockets of her pinny. Of course, not every day was a fiesta but Eduardo had always believed that as long as there were children, parents and Sunday afternoons, his 'sugar cash machine' would keep the wolf from the door.

Eduardo stretched back into the chair and lifted his right hand to block the sun from his face. He'd been feeling tired of late and it wasn't that feeling he used to get after the euphoria of the fiesta; it was a tiredness that reminded him that he was much older than his reliable 1949 Cotton Candy Machine. He took a sip of his drink, squinted and closed his eyes.

When Eduardo next looked up the table's umbrella was up and obscuring his view of the bell tower. He brought his watch to his face and saw that it was almost four. Eduardo couldn't believe it; he'd missed his first customers of the day – the children in their Sunday best. He looked over his shoulder into the bar and saw Arnau wiping the bar top and talking to two farmers perched on stools. He knew it wouldn't be long before the village would be out in force again and the steady business of candyfloss making would need to resume. But he remained at his seat outside Bar Paradiso.

For a second he closed his eyes again, but resisting, he forced them open and mopped his dripping forehead with his handkerchief and sat up straight. He looked at his cart and out to the church that he'd been baptised and married in, and where in turn Diego had been baptised. The primordial tones of the church bell struck the hour and Eduardo thought of Padre Jacob and his insistent pestering.

In the plaza a street cleaner swept the reminders of the fiesta away, children played around the fountain and a young couple walked hand in hand. Roberto had arrived with his churros stand and was serving a double helping of the doughy sticks to a fat señora in a blue dress and a white summer hat.

Eduardo thought of Arnau filling carafes of Rioja for the old farmers, and reflected that he also ought to be busy. It would take some time for the machine to warm up and for the sweet aromas to waft across the plaza. But he didn't feel like working or playing cards.

Leaving the cards on the table, Eduardo placed his hands on the arms of the chair, stiffened his back and slowly raised himself to his feet. Steadying himself, he walked over to his nearby cart, prepared himself for the creaks, massaged his hands and raised the cart onto its wheels. Eduardo pushed the cart forward and thought of his bed.

∽

EDUARDO ARRIVED AT his house and glanced up at patches of rough cement indignant against the peeling tangerine paint, before his eyes met sealed shutters. He left the cart at the front of the house and opened the front door. Climbing the dark stairway, Eduardo glanced at Diego's door with tired eyes, knowing again that he would not fling it open and throw open the shutters. He entered his own room and sat on the edge of the bed. For a few minutes he stared blankly at the far wall of the sparse room, illuminated by a candle flame of afternoon light penetrating cracks in the wooden shutter, he pulled off his shoes and rolled into the middle of the bed.

The dream disturbed his sleep again. It was always the same: a silhouetted figure of a tall youthful man wearing a Stetson hat and carrying a guitar case. The man passed through villages, towns and cities. Eduardo and his friends would always see his image from behind their cards in Bar Paradiso. Never did the man stop to take a drink or play his guitar; he strode past them before he disappeared into the distant horizon and the setting sun.

Eduardo awoke to the dark. He got up, turned the light on and, squinting, he raised his watch to his face and read it was ten minutes to twelve. He left the room, turned on the landing light, opened Diego's bedroom door and poked his head in. Diego's computer hummed and his bed was unmade. Eduardo went into the bathroom, turned the cold tap and let it run for a minute before splashing water onto his worn face. Returning to his bedroom, he opened the shutters and sat on a wooden stool. Staring into the night, Eduardo looked up at a full moon.

"Why did you have to come into my life," Eduardo heard himself saying again, "after all that time?"

Why had he stayed in the village after the war against Franco? He remembered feeling tall amongst the villagers when he first returned; they would stop him in the street and treat him like a hero. "That's when I should have gone, when I should have left Spain," Eduardo said to himself. "But where else would I have gone?"

He was just a boy, barely sixteen, and his family needed him, the village needed him. There was much to be done and there was no time for love. So when Anna Maria had arrived all those years later, Eduardo had at first been unaware of the affections of the señorita who always made a dash to his candyfloss cart after Sunday Mass. Eduardo had first come to her attention one evening, when she had been taking a late stroll with her parents past Bar Paradiso, and had heard Eduardo playing what she later described as "La musica of my love." There she had seen a man still with a young heart, and so it hadn't mattered that he was thirty years her senior, a man already in his mid-sixties. So Anna Maria had kept watering the seeds of love that she'd planted at Eduardo's cart. Before long they'd taken root. Within a year of their meeting Eduardo and Anna Maria were married and with child.

But their time together had been short, and on the day of Diego's sixth birthday Anna Maria had died; the post mortem revealed that she'd been living with a weak heart.

Eduardo's mind then turned to Diego and his friends drinking the night away, reassuring themselves in between their glugs of beer, "there are no jobs out there". His shoulders and neck muscles ached as he asked himself what had happened to that enthusiastic boy, eager to try everything and always wanting to learn a new chord or a different way to pluck the strings. But again, he couldn't answer the question and he became aware of all the sounds in the house in anticipation of the creaking door and stairs that marked Diego's return in the early hours. So Eduardo did not go back to bed; instead he went to his wardrobe and, pushing to one side a row of fading flowery dresses, he reached for the long dark neck and fine smooth curves of what had once been his substitute for love.

Eduardo sat back down on the stool, crossed his legs and gently rested the pale cypress guitar on his top leg. He ran the fingers of his left hand up the ebony fingerboard and with his free thumb he stroked the strings in a slow downward motion. He then rested his index and middle fingers on adjacent strings but as he tried to pluck them his hand cramped up and froze. Eduardo didn't try to continue. Ignoring the creaks in his back, he rose to his feet. And an ailing tone resonated around the room from the fallen guitar as Eduardo opened his lungs and cried into the night, "Qué Cabrón! Why?"

As the moon disappeared behind clouds, Eduardo made his decision. He left the room and headed downstairs to the phone.

It was only when Eduardo felt the warm paving slabs outside the Post Office that he realised he wasn't wearing his shoes. But the storm inside him swelled and he stumbled on in the night and in the direction of Bar Paradiso. On the fringes of the plaza, Eduardo fell to his knees and gasped for air. For a few moments there was nothing but darkness and silence, suddenly broken by a pulsating rhythm. Eduardo felt himself coughing and his body being pulled up by the sound. The racing beats turned to a slower, more sensual melancholia that Eduardo recognised from his past, which drew him closer to its source.

The outside of the bar was dim and the dancing gathering partially masked Eduardo's view. But he still recognized the tall outline of the man holding the guitar like a man embracing his tango partner. The familiar bittersweet music was being played by his son. It was Diego.

The crowd cried out for more but Diego shrugged his shoulders and handed the guitar back to Arnau. Eduardo took a couple of steps closer but stopped before the light of the bar revealed his presence. He stood there for a few short breaths, on the spot where he'd normally park his cart, straining his focus on Diego before he stepped back into the night and headed home.

∼

DIEGO LEANED BACK into a plastic chair, stretched out his long legs and rested them on an opposite chair. He took a long swig from a glass of beer, only pausing for a second before continuing to drink like a thirsty baby. He finished the beer and, raising his glass, called out to Arnau, who was disappearing through the beaded curtain entrance of the bar. Also slouching at the table were Javier and Ricardo.

"Diego, amigo," Ricardo said, raising his beer glass and saluting his friend. "When are you going to make your fortune and take us to Madrid?"

"Did I mention I had a cousin working there? She's got plenty of guapa friends," Javier said through a grin.

Diego mimicked a posh accent, "Anyone for tapas, and perhaps some cava to wash it down? What would I do there!?"

"Hola!" said Ricardo. "Be paid to play beautiful music, and take your pick from a million girls."

"'Cos you've been through all the ones here, amigo," snorted Javier.

"Have you ever been to Madrid before?" said Ricardo.

Arnau handed Diego another beer and between slurps, shaking his head, Diego said, "We have everything we need here!"

"Beer and sun," Ricardo said, "Yes, we have plenty of that."

"You do realise you've got a talent?" Javier said, putting his glass down and looking Diego in the eyes. "And I'm not talking about your luck with the señoritas!"

Diego turned away and took a long slurp of his beer and then, laughing, turned back and said, "Of course, but I promised Arnau I'd do a proper gig; he's gonna organise one soon. And there'll be plenty more chicas we haven't met before coming. They'll come from as far as Burgos, mark my words."

A faint drop of water landed on the bridge of Diego's nose and he cast his eyes up at dark drapes hiding the moon. Then thunder roared. At first the drops were infrequent and small and for a minute no one took much notice, but then like a drum roll the rain came continuously, and everyone dashed inside the bar. However, Diego sat there for an extra minute continuing to look up at the troubled night before he eventually escaped into the dry bar. Not long after, Arnau called time.

Dodging puddles, Diego thought to himself that at least the rain had saved him from a hangover. He gave the candyfloss cart a cursory glance as he stepped past it and slipped into the house. Diego followed the stairs up to the bathroom in the dark and his piss beat into the toilet as hard as the earlier rain. When he finished, he pulled an old metal chain that flushed the toilet, and entered his room.

Diego switched the light on. Sitting on his bed was a faded khaki coloured canvas rucksack and a sleeping bag. His shadow was caught in something that he hadn't seen in many years - his father's freshly polished Spanish guitar, propped against the bed. Diego left his bedroom and pushed open the adjacent bedroom door.

Eduardo sat up in bed and said, "Turn the light on; I've been waiting for you."

Diego switched the light on and said, "What's all that stuff doing on my bed?"

"I'm going into retirement. Now it's your turn to make your way."

"Papá, what are you talking about?"

Eduardo's dark eyes held Diego's without a blink as Eduardo said, "Fruit picking a few months a year isn't what you were put on this earth for."

Diego looked up at the ceiling to avoid his father's eyes before Eduardo said, "Come in, I want to talk to you."

Diego entered the room and sat on the end of the bed. "You know there're no jobs out there."

"It has always been like this in Spain, boom and bust. But no one's ever got a job telling themselves there're no jobs. And actually, lucky for you, there is a job waiting for you."

Diego looked blankly at his father as he continued to talk.

"Diego, I spoke to your cousin Pedro earlier and he's willing to take you on and show you the ropes; farm work isn't easy but there'll always be people to feed. You have a room waiting for you on the farm and you can start tomorrow."

Diego tried to collect his thoughts to respond to the words of his father. He didn't know what to say, and as he was thinking his father broke the silence.

"I'd heard that you weren't shy with the guitar outside of the house. But Arnau never told me people actually enjoyed your music."

"You were there, at Paradiso, tonight?"

"You won't find any working man there at the hours you keep. No, I heard you from across the plaza; in fact, I was coming to give you a good beating and to send you on your way to Pedro's farm."

Diego got to his feet and whispered to himself, "Stubborn old man," and then said, "This is loco, I'm going to bed."

Diego went to switch the light off, but he was stopped by Eduardo coughing as he said, "I'm not finished with you yet; you can switch the light off when I'm done."

Diego turned back to face his father. As he thought again about turning the light off and leaving, he saw in front of him not the face of a stubborn old man but a face of endurance. Eduardo coughed again and lifted a finger and pointed to the bed. Diego nodded and sat back down.

Eduardo cleared his throat and said, "Tonight I saw something in you, something I always kidded myself that I had – talent. Your every note moved the bar; yes, I could play, but people were never in love with my music like they loved your music tonight. And it was at that point I understood my life."

Diego wanted to correct his father but he continued to listen.

"I thought God had betrayed me, but he hadn't. I had the best years any man could have wished for with your mother and I realise that my role was never to be a guitarist. During my time selling candyfloss I made a million smiles. And I'm sorry that I stopped teaching you, made you feel guilty every time you picked up my guitar. I may have lost a wife and never come to terms with my life, but you also lost a mother and all those years you had to put up with me, and for that I'm truly sorry. But it seems you've prospered without my guidance, found your own style. I might not have been the best father but my final act is to make sure that you go out in the world and take your opportunities. So, my son, you must go away and seek your potential, because if you don't, one day you'll be old like me and still making excuses. Tomorrow you leave and it's up to you; you can go and learn how to be a farmer or you can become the best guitarist you can be. And it has to be tomorrow, before you get a chance to persuade me otherwise. You can take what you can carry on the bus and I'll make arrangements for the rest of your things."

"But Papá, there will be a time when you'll need me."

"I've never been a burden to anyone and I don't intend starting. Tomorrow I'm giving notice on this house, and with the money I save on the rent and my savings, I can afford to be in a retirement home for a few years." Eduardo reached over to the bedside table, opened its drawer and took out a framed photo of Anna Maria. He kissed the photo and then passed it to Diego. "Make sure you pack your mother safely."

"No, you're a good father. You've always been there for me; this is crazy," Diego said as he pushed the photo away. "Loco, loco."

Eduardo placed the photo on the side of the bed, rolled over to the opposite side and, pulling the bed sheets close to his face, said, "Take the photo and pack your bag."

Diego thought of all the reasons why he shouldn't go and just as he was about to list them, he heard his father snoring.

Diego took hold of the photo, switched off the light and left his father's room. For a couple of seconds he stood in the darkness of the landing and pictured the times before when his father's dark eyes had met his with the same intensity, a mad look which said he would not listen to reason. And on that basis, he entered his room and packed some clothes and the sleeping bag into the old rucksack, but he left the guitar leaning against the bed. Diego figured that it was best to follow his father's wishes that night, and within a couple of days his father would come round and show up at Pedro's farm.

Diego carried the rucksack downstairs and sat down in the front room. He looked across at the carriage clock and porcelain white stallion that had sat on the mantelpiece for as long as he could remember. His eyes moved down to the fireplace and the same old brass pokers. The grandfather clock in the hallway struck the hour of two and Diego closed his eyes. He felt the warmth of his clothes, laid out on the fireguard by his mother in winter mornings, and the cool of the fan on summer afternoons, when his father had closed the shutters and forced him to do his homework before he was allowed to play his guitar. Diego napped for a few hours before he stirred and called his father.

Eduardo arrived at the foot of the stairs wearing only a pair of old shorts, the grey hairs on his chest glistening in the early light. In one hand he held a black guitar case and in the other a wad of money and said, "Now you just need some luck."

Then he pushed forward the guitar and the money.

"Are you sure about this, Papá?"

Eduardo stuffed the money into the top pocket of Diego's dark denim shirt and placed the guitar case beside his son and then embraced Diego. Diego could still feel the warmth of his father as he opened the front door and saw the dark outlines of the barn and poplar trees lining the ridge illuminated in pinks and oranges.

2
FOOTSTEPS

Diego sat on the stone steps of the church and gazed back across the plaza in the direction of his home, before his attention was caught by the glow of Paradiso's fluorescent sign in the corner of his left eye and he turned his head towards the bar. His thoughts moved to the memory of himself as a teenager, sat alone inside the bar, plucking the strings of Arnau's guitar. He caught a glimpse of himself with Javier and Ricardo as small boys, weaving around a crowded plaza on festival day, and stopping in his tracks as his attention was caught by a bright orange balloon that had untangled itself from the clutches of a street vendor, floating away into a pastel sky.

Diego's reminiscing came to an end as his confused mind demanded an answer to his predicament. From his shirt pocket Diego took out the wad of money, removed the elastic band that bound it together, and counted through it. He thought of all the people he knew who had money, including his cousin Pedro; they were all grafters. Diego replaced the band around the notes and stuffed the wad into the back pocket of his jeans. He decided that he would catch the first bus to Pedro's farm, but first he would tune his father's guitar. He removed the old guitar from its case, plucked a string and went to work tuning it. Diego didn't see the figure approaching him and wasn't distracted until she climbed a step and stood over him.

"How far are you planning on walking today?" she asked in English.

"Cómo?" Diego said, startled.

Diego's exclamation and puzzled look were met by a girl with blue eyes, wearing a pink bandana scarf around the crown of her head and a rucksack high on her shoulders.

"You're Spanish," said the girl in Spanish, "Seventeen days of walking so far and I don't want it to end!"

"But you're not Spanish?"

"No, but I'm trying to learn Spanish."

"You learn well," Diego said.

"We Dutch are the best linguists in the world. We've got no choice; nobody speaks our stupid language! So, what's your name?"

"Diego," he said, as he leant the guitar against the church door, climbed to his feet and put out a hand. "Mucho gusto."

Shaking his hand, she said, "Nice to meet you as well; my name is Isa. So, have you seen anywhere to get a coffee? Need my caffeine and nicotine, you understand?"

Smiling, Diego gestured in the direction of Bar Paradiso and said, "Looks like the village is still sleeping."

"Well, we'd better get going to the next village, see if we can get our drugs there."

As Diego was about to explain that he was not walking The Camino de Santiago, seeking solace, spiritual enlightenment, blisters or whatever it was that all those people walking through his village sought on the pilgrim route, the sun reached over the tiled roofs at the far side of the plaza and the full beauty of Isa was revealed. Running down from her bandana, thick blonde hair curved around her cheekbones and rested in little curls on her narrow shoulders.

In her eyes Diego saw a vibrant summer's sky. Though her clothes were typical of all the backpackers that Diego had seen marching through his village - canvas trousers and a polyester shirt - they seemed to cling to her with more elegance compared to the average pilgrim. Diego thought she was similar in age to himself, perhaps twenty-one or twenty-two. Then Diego squinted as the sun blurred his vision and turned into the orange balloon from his childhood. So when Isa bent down and handed Diego his rucksack, he found himself thinking, "What the hell - the bus passes through Reliegos as well."

"Wait a minute," he said, as he removed his black Stetson from the bag. "Yes, let's get a coffee in the next village, and we can buy some smokes there as well."

As they strode across the plaza Diego noticed, dancing slightly ahead of them, elongated shadowy figures; one a trim cowboy carrying a rifle case, and the other a majorette twirling a baton.

∼

DIEGO EYED A stork building a giant nest on top of a water tower as he thought about their earlier debate. Over coffee in Reliegos Isa had told Diego the story of two lovers she'd met on the road to Santiago and the discussion centred on the premise of love at first sight. A young Italian man had originally set out on the journey with his girlfriend, but had locked eyes with a beautiful Swedish girl who was also on the walk. Every step along the road had intensified the Italian's desire for the Swedish girl. When he couldn't take it any longer he broke up with his girlfriend and then turned around and retraced his footsteps, looking for the Swedish girl who he believed was not far behind him. Within a day, the Italian had found the girl and to his joy she declared she was also in love with him. They were now engaged and upon their arrival in Santiago they planned to marry.

At first Diego hadn't believed the story. But not long after their coffee break they passed the same couple, who were ambling along the road hand in hand and seemingly in love. However, Diego said that no one was struck by a thunderbolt and fell instantly in love. He believed it was lust and while the couple would "kid themselves they were in love all the way to Santiago", afterwards they would go their own ways. Isa dismissed Diego's opinion, believing in love and "the magic of the road."

"Okay, we'll have to make a bet," Isa said. "If they marry, you pay for all my beers and smokes when we reach Santiago, and vice versa if they don't."

Diego wiped his brow with the cuff of his shirt, winked and said, "Silly Dutch girl, it'll be like taking candy from a baby," as he thought that he'd have to work his own magic soon and make his move on Isa, if he was ever to catch that bus to his cousin's farm.

"We'll see, Spanish man!" Isa said, as she smiled casually and pointed her walking stick forward in the direction of a distant church spire.

The red brick municipal albergue was the only sign of life in the village. Outside, in the first patch of green Diego had seen that day, pilgrims nestled together in different groups. Some were helping each other patch up their blistered feet; others planned the next leg of their journey and the drinkers quenched their thirst with beer and chatted like familiar locals in a bar. Diego and Isa dumped their bags on their beds and joined the drinking crowd.

The sun disappeared behind the horizon and the corn fields glowed goodbye to the day as Diego left Isa at his table.

He found himself stumbling across the garden, guitar in hand, to a table where a strawberry blonde was sitting. Two English men in the drinking crowd had spotted her and Diego promised them a lesson in Spanish charm.

"Hola señorita, you speak Spanish?"

The strawberry blonde folded her book but avoided eye contact with Diego.

"Si,"

"But I believe you're American, si?"

"Very perceptive."

"But you know Spanish?"

"Let's just say I'm learning about the Spanish!" she replied.

The woman reopened her book. However, it had become too dark to read, and she closed the book and turned her head to face Diego. Diego then noticed she had a scar on the right side of her face; starting close to the right edge of her eye, it ran along her cheekbone and disappeared at the edge of her top lip. Diego staggered and balanced against his guitar.

Trying his best to look away from the scar, Diego said, "Why are you walking the Camino?"

"If we become friends, then you can ask me that question."

Diego searched his head for a better line before the woman broke the silence: "So can you play that guitar of yours, or is it just a leaning post?"

Diego steadied himself, placed his right arm under the belly of his guitar and drew it to his hip. "Of course I can play it; I'm going to play something special for you."

Looking him up and down, she said, "I grew up around men with big hats and guitars, so I'm not easily impressed. Hope you're good!"

"They come from miles to hear me play," Diego said as he winked and widened his stance.

The blonde's guarded face turned to an ecstatic smile as Diego's first chord softened the night and the notes formed a melody of serenity and love. As Diego lifted the tempo, he imagined the lady in a black dress lifting her long sandy hair into a tangled ball above her head and then letting it fall gently over her eyes as she swayed to his music. Diego then lifted a foot onto a chair and leaned closer in to her.

Diego woke to the smell of bleach and the image of a plump bottom attached to a woman mopping the floor. He squirmed out of bed, sat on the edge and sank his head into his hands. His eyes travelled down a long tunnel. Every time he tried to think about the night before the end of the tunnel darkened. Diego gave up the fight with his memory and looked up at the rows of empty bunks, estimating the room could sleep fifty or so. He gripped the hand rail of the bed above, pulled himself up and grabbed his jeans off the floor.

Diego sat in the empty garden; watching swallows dancing around the spire of a nearby church. He drew deeply on a cigarette. Beating away a fly from the rim of his cup, he drank the remains of his sweet coffee and lit another cigarette but was still no closer to deciding whether to catch a bus in the direction of Pedro's farm, or catch up with Isa and continue walking the journey west for a little longer. He searched his trouser pockets and thought about texting Ricardo and explaining his disappearance and his possible pursuit of a "delicioso Dutch chica", but all he found was some loose change. He reached into the top pocket of his shirt but found it was also empty. Sitting up straight, Diego adjusted his hat higher onto his head, and stiffened like a focused cat. Then he sprang out of his chair.

Diego found his backpack and guitar where he'd left them by the bunk. He searched the pockets of the bag before emptying its contents onto the floor; everything was there, including the framed photo of his mother, all apart from his money and his mobile phone. He glanced up to see the cleaner walking with authority towards him.

"You know everyone left hours ago, at the crack of dawn," the woman said, as she looked at Diego's pile of stuff on the floor.

"My money and my cellular, gone - they've been stolen!"

"Let's not jump to any conclusions; after all, I nearly told them to put you in the hammock last night, the state you were in! Okay, when did you last see your money and phone?"

"Some people put me to bed?" Diego asked, "Who put me to bed?"

"That crowd you were with and that girl, Dutch I think she was."

Diego readjusted his hat and said, "Well, it's her then! I should have my head read, stupid Spanish man; she would have seen my money. She was playing me from the first minute she laid eyes on me."

"You'd be wise not to trust everyone you meet on the road, but as I said, don't rush into making a judgment. Take a deep breath and give yourself a moment."

Ignoring the advice, Diego shouted, "Puta!" and began stuffing his things back into his rucksack. He said, "I'm just amazed she didn't take my guitar as well!"

"I can call the police if you like, but I suggest you keep your foul language to yourself."

"It's okay, you don't need to do that; I'll sort this out myself. But I can only pay you this," Diego showed the woman his remaining loose change.

Playing with the loose change in his pocket, Diego followed the westerly pointing yellow arrow painted on a stone marker with 335 KM carved into it.

CANDYFLOSS GUITAR

~

DIEGO IGNORED THE customary pilgrim greeting of "buen camino" from the old man with a strange accent and staff-like walking stick, who passed him like an explorer on the ascending trail. Instead he looked down at his boots and the many footprints in the dirt path, wondering which brand of walking boots Isa had been wearing. Then he removed his hat from his head, let it dangle round the back of his olive neck and tied his black hair into a ponytail. Diego continued to climb, his pace outwardly set by the slow whirs of an out-of-sight wind turbine.

At the hill's brow three pilgrim backpackers were sitting against the stone wall of a hermitage, enjoying lunch and conversation. As had been Diego's custom all day, he chose to keep himself to himself, and took a seat on a crumbling ridge sliced open by slate stones. To the north, rows of wind turbines ran across overlapping hills like a domino run. To the east he saw a golden valley with hay bales stacked like ancient defences, overlooked by red hills. It was a land that Diego had passed through for the last day and a half and yet he didn't remember its detail. He felt he was looking at a painting with no name or context.

He removed a chorizo bocadillo from his rucksack. It was only after he'd eaten the baguette that he remembered that he had earlier told himself to save at least half of it. He lit a cigarette and for a few minutes his thoughts were blank. Then the mountain rain came and the painting disappeared behind a misty veil.

Diego followed the yellow arrows along ancient Roman roads that made for easy walking. He spent the night on the floor of a Sunday School classroom with a jovial bunch of South Koreans who wanted to talk football. But Diego didn't care to talk and sat through the communal dinner with a vacant look, like a hobo in a lodging house for tramps. Diego's roommates were still sleeping when he got up, so he made a quick dash for the exit, only slowed down by the cursory glance he gave to a donation box and handwritten sign asking pilgrims to leave only what they could afford. Diego fumbled with the remaining change in his pocket but remembered he was running low on smokes.

As the day faded, Diego strayed into a large city and followed a stream of people through the city's bustling alleys, until one opened into the main plaza. He sat down on a bench in the shadows of a towering gothic cathedral, removed his boots and rubbed his feet. Feeling hungry and thirsty, he looked up at the busy cafes and tourists enjoying the pleasures of a drink in the final patches of sunlight and thought, "Just one more day, that's all I'll need to catch that Dutch bitch; then I'll be back home enjoying a beer in Paradiso."

He also caught himself watching a group of old men wearing cotton shirts tucked deeply into their dark trousers and pot-belly waists, sitting on a bench under the only tree in the plaza, making hand gestures and no doubt talking nostalgically. And it was then that he realised he'd been carrying his father's guitar and yet he couldn't remember taking it out of its case. He put his boots on and removed the instrument from the protection of the hard case that had been trailing by his side. Then he saw the broken string and splinted tuning key and his memory from his first night on the road was restored.

He remembered that he'd started well enough before his enthusiasm and the beers betrayed him. Picking hard on an E string, he'd raised his eyes towards the blonde's eyes, but just as he'd been about to conclude his trademark move with the lyrically timed words of "beautiful dancer", it hadn't been the blonde who was moved, but Diego's feet. He had felt as if a tablecloth was being badly whisked away from underneath him and he'd found himself in a mute world, looking up at an indigo sky.

Grimacing, Diego returned the injured guitar to its case, got to his feet and headed towards the old men under the tree. After several minutes of debate, one man led Diego out of the square and through cobbled alleys sliding down a hill, until they arrived outside a small shop with a fading sign that instantly grabbed Diego's attention: Taller de Guitarras. Outside a man was securing a shutter with a padlock, hiding the shop's window. The man took a few seconds to stand straight and he met his visitors with a pained expression. Diego could see he was short, and his rounded shoulders and crooked stance made him appear even shorter; in Diego's mind the man was five-feet-four or less. The old man who'd taken Diego to the workshop warmly placed a hand on Diego's right shoulder and said goodbye, leaving Diego to introduce himself to the proprietor.

Reaching out with his free hand, Diego went to shake the man's hand and said, "Mucho gusto, I need a new tuning key and string for my guitar."

The crooked man responded with a sniffle. "Can't you see I've just closed? You'll have to come back in two days when I'm open again."

"Señor, please, it's a matter of urgency that I get it fixed tonight. And I'll make it worth your while, but it'll be a few days before I'd be able to pay you."

"Now you're just wasting my time, cash up front or nothing," said the man as he turned to leave.

As the man took a step away, Diego placed a hand on the back of his right shoulder and said, "You don't understand - it's my father's guitar and I've damaged it."

The man stopped and thought for a moment before turning round to face Diego. Quietly he said, "Show me this guitar of your father's."

Diego removed the guitar from its case and presented it to the old man. The man removed a monocle attached with some string to the inside of his shirt pocket, raised his right half-grey eyebrow and fitted the circular lens around his eye. He took the guitar and cradled it in his arms. Drawing the guitar closer to the monocle, he placed a hand on the bridge and felt the tension of the remaining strings and ran his hand down its errant patterned body to a small abrasion on its side.

"This is your father's guitar?"

"That's what I said."

"He's had it a long time?"

"I believe he bought it with the money he earned as a Republican soldier."

The old man handed the guitar back to Diego and slowly knelt down to the base of the shop's shutter, removed a bunch of keys from his pocket and unlocked the padlock. Turning to Diego, he said, "Where's your manners boy, can't you see I'm an old man?"

Diego didn't need to be asked again; he leaned the guitar against a flickering lamppost, squatted down and eased the shutter up.

The old man unlocked the door to his shop and as he did, he said, "I can tell you exactly where he bought the guitar, and maybe even the year."

Diego, with the guitar in hand, followed the luthier into his dark workshop. The air was heavy with sawdust and he dodged a number of guitars in various stages of production, hanging on hooks. Leaning against one wall were stacks of different wood, which Diego guessed were from distant places. At a workbench the man drew up a stool and rolled up his sleeves, and Diego handed him the guitar.

"He bought it in Jose Ramirez's guitar shop in Madrid; they manufacture the best guitars in all of Spain and, when your father bought it, the best guitars in the world. The serial number no longer remains but judging by the age of the wood, I'd agree it's from the time of the war. Perhaps he bought it to make his fellow comrades cheery. Either way, it survived a war, and this bruising is recent."

The luthier picked up his tools and went to work on the guitar and, like an artist lost in his work, he didn't give Diego an opportunity to respond, which suited Diego fine. Within an hour the guitar was repaired, there was no sign of the abrasion and the body glowed like the coat of a champion horse. And its sixth string had been replaced by a steel string.

The luthier pushed the guitar towards Diego but Diego hesitated, "Please, you demonstrate this new string."

However, the luthier continued to hold the guitar for Diego and said, "A luthier makes guitars and a guitarist plays guitars."

"You've really saved my ass, muchas gracias. But as I said, it will be a few days before I can pay."

The man raised his eyebrows and through a half-smile said, "It's not often a guitar makes me reopen the shop at the end of the day. It's on the house."

Diego received the guitar and plucked the new string, producing a low tone that seemed to waft the sawdust and make the shadows in the room shudder.

∼

STANDING IN THE cathedral's long shadow, Diego placed his hat on the floor. He first played a classic that he'd learnt as a child, *'Romance Anonimo'*, and as the sweet notes were exchanged for the odd coin Diego's confidence grew, and he switched to his trademark gypsy rhythms. To Diego's surprise a small crowd formed around him and a few listeners appeared blind, fixated in the moment, swaying their heads from side to side. Diego made enough money to eat in a cheap restaurant. But unable to find an inexpensive bed for the night, he wandered the streets until he found a small empty plaza lined on its south side by a medieval arcade. He rolled his sleeping bag out under the arches and bedded in for the night.

Diego wasn't sure how long he'd been asleep when he felt a presence above him; instinctively, he sat up in his sleeping bag. His blurry eyes saw a vision of a man shaking a bottle of something above his head.

"What the hell do you want?"

Shaking the bottle again, the stranger said, "Sorry Señor, excuse me. Were you asleep?"

The man appeared stocky and well-supported by legs as solid as tree stumps. His grey flecks in a semi-kept beard sparkled against chestnut eyes.

"Yes, I was! Now get out of here and leave me alone; I'm no wino."

"Suit yourself; I'll just make myself comfortable the other side of the plaza and share my drink with God, in that case," whispered the man.

The man retired to the other side of the plaza and rolled out a sleeping bag. Diego tried to keep an eye on him but it was too arduous due to the darkening night and his exhausted body.

The next morning the unwelcome guest was gone and Diego's reluctant legs were only roused by the chatter of passing pilgrims and the thought of Isa with his father's fiesta money. As Diego passed through an ancient gateway in a walled part of the city, he was stopped by a gypsy woman offering a bunch of herbs and promising to tell Diego his future. Diego automatically dismissed her. A minute later though, to his own surprise, Diego found himself back at the gateway pushing the remains of his busking money into the hard hands of the gypsy, although he still resisted her offer to tell his fortune.

Diego passed through pregnant vineyards, olive groves and orchards, connected by long solitary dry stretches. And when he strayed into a village that appeared to have some life he'd busk and play his usual repertoire of songs. Always he drew a small crowd and his hat filled with enough money for food and a bed.

One afternoon Diego took a break on a stone wall next to a pastured field with a flock of sheep huddled together and began writing a mental list of the pros and cons of being a farmhand. Just as Diego was figuring that if he went to Pedro's straight away and gave up drinking for a while, it wouldn't be long before he'd save the equivalent of the stolen money, he was disturbed by a shepherd sitting side saddle on a donkey.

"Mucho sol, amigo, it's very hot today, no?" said the shepherd.

He leaned over and offered Diego a leather hip flask. Without much thought, Diego accepted the flask, undid its lid and closed his eyes as cold water massaged the back of his throat.

"Gracias," Diego said, opening his eyes.

"Still a long way to Santiago!" said the shepherd.

"What makes you think I'm going to Santiago?"

"Why, aren't you? I must admit, you don't really look like the walking type. So what brings you out here then? Counting sheep is no way to pass the day!" said the shepherd, laughing.

"Not sure, I was thinking about farm work,"

"There's no romance in farm work," replied the shepherd as he nodded at the guitar case propped against the wall. "You play well?"

"It depends who you ask," Diego mumbled.

"Well, I'd stick to the guitar, don't reckon farming would suit you."

"What makes you say that?"

"You don't look like a farmer," responded the shepherd matter-of-factly.

"I've been around farms. In fact, my cousin has a cattle farm; it's been in the family for generations."

"You a morning person then?" said the shepherd through a grin.

"If I had to be, why not? Hard work never did my father any harm, and my cousin and his family are doing alright."

"I love being a shepherd," said the man as he placed two fingers in his mouth and whistled a sharp shrill that summoned a black and white border collie chasing a sheep from a further field. "Funny, it's always that same damn sheep that never wants to stay with the flock."

The shepherd prodded the donkey with his right heel.

"Your water," Diego shouted, waving the flask at the departing shepherd.

"It's a hot summer, make sure you drink plenty."

The shepherd then looked back and shouted, "Keep walking down the lane and when you get to the end you'll see a stile; climb over and take a path to the right that crosses a field. It will put you a couple of hours ahead on the Camino."

Diego's eyes followed the flock of sheep and the reluctant sheep trailing at the back until they disappeared through a gate into a distant field.

Throughout the afternoon Diego had the feeling he was being followed. But every time he looked over his shoulder there was no one there. After walking through a wood of eucalyptus trees, the trail opened into a meadow, home to a dominating cypress tree. Diego thought he heard a twig snap behind him and he turned round and shouted back into the trees, "Who's there?" But all he heard was his echo.

When Diego turned back, the enormity of the tree struck him. Its trunk was as sturdy as a Roman pillar and its crown was bathed in thick green foliage. He walked up to the tree and ran his hand across its rough bark, and was reminded of his father's hand. Looking up, Diego had an idea. He removed his rucksack and hid it with his guitar behind the trunk, and proceeded to climb the tree. About a fifth of the way up, at a large knot, a branch the size of a dugout canoe extended and beckoned Diego. He crawled along it, propped his back against the tree's spine and tipped his hat over his eyes. It wasn't long before he was asleep.

∽

WHEN HE AWOKE, a small A-frame tent was pitched under the tree. Sitting outside the tent, cross-legged in the last patch of sunlight, was a man boiling a pan of water on a small gas burner. Diego recognised him straight away – it was the bearded man who had dangled a bottle in front of his sleepy eyes some three nights ago.

Just as Diego was wondering how he might climb down the tree and avoid the man's attention, the man looked up and said, "I'm making coffee; you need a hand down?"

"No thanks. I was just trying to see how far it was to the next village," Diego said foolishly, as he pointed across ploughed fields and the horizon, edging his way round on his knees to face the trunk of the tree. "Don't think it's too far."

"Well, just shout if you fall," quipped the bearded man as he leaned over the gas burner and poured boiling water into two mugs.

Diego dropped behind the tree, heaved his rucksack onto his back and lifted the guitar case. Walking towards the man, who was now standing and holding both mugs in separate hands, Diego paused for a brief second. No sooner had Diego stopped than the man pushed forward a mug.

Keeping his hands by his side, Diego said, "Have you been following me?"

Laughing, the man replied, "I've been following you, you've been following the pilgrims in front of you, and they've been following in the footsteps of a million more pilgrims before them."

Screwing his face up, Diego thought of the reluctant sheep.

"It's only instant coffee, but I'm told it tastes better with this," said the man as he balanced both mugs in one hand and with his free hand removed a small bottle of rum from inside his fleece; he proceeded to top up both coffees with its contents. "This'll help you on your way," said the bearded man through a grin, as he once again offered the mug.

Diego met the gesture with the eyes of a curious fox, and as a light breeze whistled through the treetops Diego said, "Well, it can't do any harm," and accepted the drink. "My father swears by it."

The bearded man raised his mug at Diego and said, "To your old man then!"

Diego met the man's cup with his own and they both took a hearty drink.

"Well, as we're having aperitifs, you'll join me for dinner, won't you?"

"I did want to see about getting a bus..."

"Have you ever tasted fresh rabbit?" interrupted the man, as he poured more rum into Diego's mug.

∼

IN THE LIGHT of the fire, the man reminded Diego of a dwarf from the fantasy books he used to read as a child; he had wide shoulders strong enough to carry a tree, and large hands made for brandishing a solid tool. The dwarf-like man tossed the remains of a bone into the fire and took a toothpick to his mouth. During dinner Diego learned his story.

Leonardo came from a small village in the Basque region. He had not worked in three years since losing his job in construction and was broke after his state benefits had come to an end. He had travelled all around his region looking for work but to no avail, and more or less had been a kept man, living at his girlfriend's place. Many men in Leonardo's village were in a similar situation. However, Leonardo had managed to keep himself relatively busy by doing the odd job here and there in return for payment in some form, such as eggs, ham, paint or a drink. He believed modern capitalism would collapse and trade would return to the barter system. Diego could feel that Leonardo had suffered, and he tried to top up Leonardo's cup with rum. But Leonardo pulled his mug away and tipped the remains of his drink into the fire, and that's when he admitted to Diego that his drinking habit had nearly finished him off.

Leonardo had found himself in the early hours on the roof of a house, in a ghost town of a housing estate, where he'd last worked. He was drunk as a skunk and was heaving off roof tiles in the hope that he might be able to sell them.

When he'd dropped one of the slate tiles, and the sound of its shattering pieces pierced his body like the stabbing of a knife, it was then that he'd decided to kill himself. The next thing Leonardo remembered was standing on the edge of the ridge that hung over his village like an evil force. He held his eyes shut and counted to himself as he lifted one foot towards the abyss. But just as he was about to take a step, he heard the call of an owl, and he found his eyes free, focusing on a map of stars. The Milky Way glowed in front of Leonardo like cats' eyes in the night and depicted a road arching westward. Then the faint tones of the village church bells rang and echoed, "Santiago, Santiago". A few hours later Leonardo had packed his rucksack, left a note for his girlfriend and was marching uphill and westward, wondering who he might meet on his pilgrimage.

When Leonardo stopped playing with his toothpick, he smiled and said, "You've come this far, and now you're going to take the bus home. Don't you feel the path of change?"

Diego lit himself a cigarette and offered one to Leonardo, who gratefully accepted, before Diego eventually answered, "I told you, I'm not walking to Santiago; I was just trying to unravel another one of my fuck ups," Diego took a long drag and continued, "But I have to accept I'm not going to see the money or that Dutch girl again. So no, I don't feel any change, but perhaps I am accepting what life is like – sometimes you have to know when to let go and get on with it. So I'm going to learn farming and make my own way in the world, just like my father did – that's what I've realised."

"I understand all that, but maybe you're on a certain path at the moment whether you like it or not; perhaps it's better to complete it first and then see how you feel. What I'm learning is the Camino to Santiago is like life condensed into a very small period, where you see its many facets – you have the chance to walk slowly and consider it. Do you understand what I'm saying?"

Diego poked the fire with a stick and replied, "Not really, but I'm listening."

"What about the relationships made on the Camino? Some may be brief, others more permanent, but all such relationships will experience hurdles; or I could talk about the challenges reaching Santiago – success is never plain sailing." Leonardo stroked the hairs on his chin and looked beyond the fire at the shadows dancing on the girth of the cypress tree.

"But let me tell you about something that has profoundly affected me. I used to work with a lot of wood, but really it was no longer wood; its core beauty and strength were destroyed. Wood is mixed with alien things and fabricated for the purpose of building as cheaply as possible. I'd forgotten how as a child I used to roam the woods, climb the trees and feel lost but safe in a magic kingdom. Now those forests surrounding my village no longer exist. But here on The Camino I feel the trees again – they breathe, they sigh, they talk and sometimes they cry. We don't need to butcher them; when their old limbs are dying we need to prune them and later we need to cut them back to their bases and prepare them for rebirth. In short, we need to return to the old ways of managing the forests. They can serve us and we can serve them. I know upon the completion of my journey to Santiago I will work with trees; I don't know exactly how, but I believe the road will give me the answer."

Diego stretched out across the grass, looked up at the night.

"I'm happy for you." Momentarily Diego's attention was caught by a shooting star skimming across the night's sky, before its bright light faded and dissolved into the abyss. "But what if one doesn't have that eureka moment, what if we are just one of a million stars, lost without any purpose?"

Leonardo smiled and said, "Each and every one of those stars above us has a purpose. And your purpose, I believe, is right under your nose and you don't even see it!"

"You reckon!"

"How many times have you wished you were carrying less? I know I've dumped a few things on the way. And you, you carry that big guitar case in addition to your backpack. Surely it's a massive handicap, no?"

"Yes, but it's my father's, he gave it to me. What else am I supposed to do with it?"

"If you really didn't want to carry it, you would have found a way to lose it by now. So let's not bullshit any more – you carry it because you don't want to let go of your dreams. But at the same time you're too scared to share your dreams. You think if you do, you'll be ridiculed. But people will never achieve their dreams unless they truly commit to them. That's why since we've been sitting here tonight you haven't once offered to play for me!"

"But it's just you and me out here in the middle of nowhere."

"Am I not a big enough audience? Besides, don't you ever play for yourself?"

Diego acknowledged this with a small nod and said, "I used to, all the time."

Diego poked the fire with his stick and a yellow flame the shape of a poplar tree emerged from a white ember. Leonardo stood up and threw the stub of his cigarette into the fire. He walked over to the tent, retrieved Diego's guitar from its case and ran a hand down one of its sides, then he put his nose in the sound hole and closed his eyes for a few moments before handing the instrument to Diego.

Diego took a drag on his cigarette, then tossed it into the fire and took the guitar. He sat upright and crossed his legs.

Diego shivered and said, "Okay, if you really want me to, but don't expect too much, I think that rum's gone to my head."

He reached for his hat from the grass, adjusted it so the rim hung halfway over his eyes, and looked down at the guitar, which he held close to his chest. He tenderly stroked the strings with his middle fingers and the music that emerged was like the sound of a small brook flowing with ease. But suddenly clouds burst and Diego's hand raced up and down the neck of the guitar and the brook was now a torrent of water, being hit by a rain storm; a fast-paced Latino sounding rumba danced around the meadow. Diego tilted his head back, locked his jaws and closed his eyes. The storm reached a crescendo; a pluck on the strings suggested an abrupt end, as a note resonated in the air. However, before the note died, the brook began to find its way and flow more gently. Diego slowly caressed the strings of the guitar with the gentleness of a lover and the water bobbled around pebbles and raindrops fell lightly and rhythmically onto the brook.

Diego felt the wind on his face; he relaxed his jaws and opened his eyes. The flames of the fire appeared to arch to one side, revealing the faint outline of an old man standing on the path of The Camino. The old man then raised a cup of something in Diego's direction. Abruptly the wind changed direction and the man was gone. Diego laid the guitar by his side, rubbed his eyes and looked over to his left where Leonardo was still sitting but with his sleeping bag now wrapped around his upper body. And then the leaves of the cypress tree began to shake, producing a high-pitched romantic whistle in the breeze.

Leonardo clapped loudly and cheered, "Bravo, bravo, but why did you stop? The tree, it wants to sing, it wants to sing!"

3
ALL ROADS LEAD SOMEWHERE

The next day Diego and Leonardo met an athletic-looking man who knew many uses for the flora along the road to Santiago. They met him in the shade of an apple orchard where he was meditating bare-chested next to his stall of biscuits, fruits and juices. Diego noticed that a scallop shell hung around his neck and he remembered he'd seen other pilgrims with scallop shells fastened to their backpacks. As soon as Diego and Leonardo arrived, the man opened his eyes and insisted they sit down and help themselves to refreshments. Diego and Leonardo didn't need to be asked twice. The man introduced himself as Juan and said he'd been a policeman in a former life and now spent his time walking the Camino, assisting the pilgrims. And when Leonardo mentioned his passion for trees, Juan began to talk about all the various medicines and ointments that could be extracted from the local flora.

Naturally, Leonardo was keen to learn as much as possible and so gratefully accepted Juan's offer of dinner and a pitch for the night at his nearby shack. Diego, on the other hand, was keen to press on to the next town before the day faded.

Diego and Leonardo embraced each other with the love of brothers and agreed that if they did not catch up in Santiago, they would no doubt meet again sometime. It also felt natural that Diego should receive a goodbye hug from Juan.

After what seemed a lifetime to Diego, Juan let go of his grip and said, "So, Mariachi, you never did say why you're walking the Camino?"

Diego looked over towards Leonardo but Leonardo was cross-legged and napping under an apple tree.

"Until you define your reason, it will still just be a walk," said Juan, grabbing Diego's attention again.

Diego looked back at the path he had just taken and then looked west as it disappeared into a rich orange twilight on the horizon.

He picked up his guitar case by its handle and raised it up to Juan's eyeline and said, "As soon as I accepted this from my father, I had my reason for my pilgrimage." And with that Diego tipped his hat, smiled and said, "Never been one for saying much, let my music do my talking."

Later that evening when Diego rolled into another medieval town, he found there were no beds left at the pilgrims' hostel. But as he stood outside and dug into his pockets for his cigarettes, he pulled out a fifty Euro note with his box of cigarettes. That night Diego slept in a comfortable bed in a hotel room overlooking the main plaza, thinking this would probably be the first and last time that he was ever likely to meet a saint.

∼

AS DIEGO WALKED, lyrics came with ease. Each time he stopped to busk, a willing audience always gathered. And one evening as he played to a gathering in a small plaza, his dreamy eyes looked out to a packed audience in Madrid's Estadio Bernabeu.

A week later Diego arrived in Sarria, a bustling little junction town of pilgrims. Diego chose a spot opposite an Italian restaurant, named Federico's, on a narrow street that formed the Camino and snaked its way upwards towards the remains of a medieval tower.

Diego tilted his guitar under his right arm and began strumming at fast pace a song that had come to him that morning.

Don't be scared to love again
Don't be chicken-shit
If you're a matador reveal your cape,
A queen your feathered wings.
A bee is a bee,
A grape is a grape
Me, I'm a Flamenco guy
So my dear Señora, stamp your feet and
throw my dinner to the sky.

We'll always share the sun, the moon,
the distant stars
But remember when I come home
I'm your Flamenco guy...

It seemed that everyone who made their way up the hill stopped and found the passion of Flamenco; surrounding Diego, they clapped their hands in time with the beat and greeted Diego's sweeps of his hat with cheers of "Olé, Olé!" Diego played off the energy of the crowd and at that moment he felt he could accomplish anything. So he didn't pay too much attention to the feeling of bubbles rising through his head; instead, he mopped his sweating brow with the cuff of his shirt and looked up to a radiant sun smiling back at him.

Swallows chased around San Pedro's spire before the view was blocked by a blurred image of a woman, bending down, and resting a motherly hand under Diego's head. Diego then felt cool drops of water on his lips, which he touched with his tongue. Opening blurry eyes, Diego saw he was encircled by anxious pilgrims. Kneeling above him, a woman with long dark hair and a kind smile held a bottle of water to his mouth.

"You need to learn to pace yourself; now take small sips," said the woman.

"And by the way, thanks for the music; you've been fantastic for business," said a man with a goatee, who knelt down and joined the woman.

Diego tried to find some words as he was led through the doorway of the Italian restaurant, but nothing came.

A banquet atmosphere filled the restaurant and bombarded Diego's senses. Squashed along communal oak tables, customers feasted on dishes of pasta, lasagne, pizza and other Italian dishes that Diego didn't know the name of. The woman with the long hair joined a younger waitress who also had long dark hair, although her hair spanned the full length of her back, and the two slim waitresses spun around the tables like dancers.

Diego stumbled across the restaurant and was seated at a square table at the back. Hanging behind him, a vintage metal poster advertised Martini from Turin. Moments after, the younger of the waitresses, who Diego reckoned was in her early thirties, deposited a jug of iced water and two glasses on the table. The man with the goatee drew up a seat opposite Diego.

"My name is Federico, benvenuto," he said, smiling and reaching out a hand, "and the beautiful signora who helped you in is my wife Isabel."

"Mucho gusto; Diego. I think I passed out or something," Diego said as he faintly shook Federico's hand and tried to read the man's intentions.

"Yes, that's the long and short of it. You really have to look after yourself in the heat, especially on this stretch of the Camino," Federico said sagely. "But don't worry, you'll be all right." Federico poured Diego a glass of water. "That girl who just brought the water, Angela is her name; she's Italian but she never learnt to cook! Funny, one morning I was about to put a note in the window to advertise for help and I saw her lying in the same spot that we picked you up. Don't know what I'd do without her now, but when she's ready she'll move on."

Federico's gestures danced with passion as he moved on to his own history. Diego learned that Federico was from Milan and all he ever wanted to be was a chef and own a restaurant. However, lady luck had not gone Federico's way in Italy. He explained that in Italy, restaurants stayed within families and so there was never an opportunity for Federico to buy an ongoing business. Or when premises became available, the banks were never kind to Federico. One night, exhausted after running a kitchen that had served a feast to a convention of drunken bankers, Federico squared up to his unappreciative boss, the owner of the catering company, and asked him if he could invest in his business. The boss had inherited wealth and position but unfortunately not benevolence. Laughing smugly, the boss said that Federico should know his place and be grateful for having such a job. Federico's reaction was to land a serving tray of tiramisu over his boss's head!

Federico found himself walking the streets of Milan before he eventually stopped at a canal. Leaning over the canal's railings, he wondered how he was going to explain his actions to Isabel. But the water was dark and provided no answers.

So Federico resumed his wanderings before the dim light of an empty bar offered asylum.

Diego doused his forehead with ice as Federico's tempo picked up and he said, throwing his arms in the air, "That's when I met my guardian angel; we all have one, you know. Mine is a Pole named Jarek." Jarek was the barman in the empty bar and had walked the road to Santiago, and that night he had told Federico his story.

Federico and Isabel never made it to Santiago, though that had been their intention when they had started out on the road some two years ago. Upon reaching Sarria, with just some 100km left to reach Santiago's cathedral, they'd both felt something that at the time they couldn't explain or understand, "Invisible bubbles - a strange energy", that made them feel light-headed and stopped them in their tracks outside a sorry state of a building. The building was roofless and falling down but Federico and Isabel didn't see a ruined building; they saw something else. It turned out the town council was giving grants to people willing to take on derelict buildings and return them to a state of grace. And so *Federico's* was born.

Federico's arms finally rested by his side when he ended his story, and leaning back in his chair he said, "So I have a proposition for you, Flamenco guy." Pausing for a second, he stroked his goatee before continuing, "How about you play some gigs here? In return I can offer you a bed and Italian cooking lessons and, of course, you get to keep any tips you make."

Diego took a swig of water, "That's a nice offer, maybe the best offer someone's ever given me," Diego smiled. "Well, nearly! But I'm keen to get to Santiago, you understand. But it's a fantastic restaurant."

"If you're in a hurry to get to Santiago, don't let me hold you back. But there would be no obligation to stay for a certain time."

"It's a decent bed?"

"Of course, it was shipped over from Italy!"

"Tempting, very tempting! You have Spanish beer as well?"

"Spanish people," Federico said, shaking his head and smiling as he leaned across the table to shake Diego's hand, "As much Spanish beer as you like. We have a deal, then?"

∽

DURING THE DAY Diego worked in the kitchen, learning to cook pasta "al dente"; he also learned that "less is more" and that "all the best food (as well as the best-looking women, footballers, fashion etc.) comes from Italy!" At night he put extra tables and chairs in the street before he performed. The songs came easily; sometimes Diego improvised and at other times he experimented with some of his old favourites.

One night after another busy evening Diego was sitting outside alone smoking a cigarette and thumbing through a wad of money, his reward for his evening's performance. He folded the bank notes and placed the pile in his shirt pocket, and then all of sudden he thought of his father. Diego stepped into the restaurant, picked up the phone behind the counter and tapped in a number. But the phone didn't ring; instead Diego heard a sharp three-beat tone suggesting the phone line had been disconnected. He put the handset down and took a deep breath and then dialed another number.

After many rings, he finally heard a familiar voice on the line, "Hola Catalan, guess who?" Diego said into the phone.

Arnau spoke with relief and urgency. Diego learned he'd lost his mobile phone in Bar Paradiso the night of his performance, before Arnau said he had some very bad news for him.

Diego paused for a long moment, and went to put the handset down. But he composed himself and said, "It's strange, I don't know why now, but all of a sudden I felt I needed to speak to Papá. He's died?"

Arnau then told Diego that his father had died the day Diego had disappeared. Feeling dizzy Diego told Arnau that he would call him back first thing the next morning. He put the phone down and stepped into the street. Diego cried silently in the dark. He cried for his father but most of all he cried for himself. He knew his journey was over. Diego looked up at the night's sky, illuminated by a network of phosphorescent opportunities, closed his eyes and tried to make sense of everything. Then he felt the earth beneath him move; he reached for a chair before he passed out.

∾

DIEGO AWOKE TO a sweet aroma floating around the room. He pulled himself out of the comfortable bed and opened the shutters. A full moon lit the lane outside Federico's restaurant and the scent appeared to be coming from further up the hill.

Diego fumbled around the room for his clothes and within minutes he found himself outside on the quiet street. The smell intensified and he followed the aroma up the hill and towards the tower.

The smell was familiar and yet Diego couldn't quite place it. He thought for a moment it might be a strong perfume and then he was reminded of some of the flowers he'd experienced on his journey. But when he reached the top of the hill and saw a familiar sight in front of the ancient tower, his curiosity was answered. Mists of pink clouds spun around in a machine that was being worked with a steady pride.

"Diego, yes it's me, Papá. Don't be alarmed," Eduardo whispered. "Now take a seat," he continued as he pointed to a nearby bench, "and tell me about your adventures."

"Don't think I was drinking and I'm pretty sure I'm not dreaming. So it really is you - what are you doing out here?" Diego said as he turned his attention to the machine.

"They don't make them like that anymore," Eduardo said, smiling.

"Christ, this is loco, you died?" Diego stammered as he slumped into the bench.

"I must be dreaming; either that or I have truly lost it,"

"You are fine, my boy, although you did have a fever and I believe the kind Italians have been nursing you back to health for the last couple of days. But yes, my time for living in this world recently came to an end."

Diego closed his eyes momentarily but when he reopened them, Eduardo was still there and pouring pink coloured sugar into his machine.

"But here you are?"

"I'm just visiting, to say goodbye. The police were trying to track you down. So I thought it was best if I came to see you myself."

"You had a funeral?"

"The biggest the village has seen in a long time," Eduardo said through a smile. "I departed the morning you left the village. And on that very same day, just after Padre Jacob was told the news, a blonde American woman with a scar on her face came into the church and handed him a large bundle of cash."

Eduardo went on to explain that the mystery blonde had been taking a rest on the church's steps and found the money there - the wad of notes that had once been in Diego's hand. She then felt compelled to make her confession.

"Padre Jacob even believes the money was a donation from God for me! Can you believe that? But maybe returning the money for my funeral was divine intervention; I'm not sure, I still have a lot to learn." Eduardo grinned and continued, "They even unveiled a little plaque for me outside of Paradiso, followed by a festival. You can imagine how happy that made Arnau! Now tell me about your road to Santiago. You know, you're the first in the village to make the pilgrimage."

"No no, this is loco, I must be dreaming or hallucinating or something! If anyone came up here they'd have me committed; you're not here," Diego said as he clambered to his feet.

At that moment Eduardo dipped a stick into the drum of the machine and ran it around its spinning edge to create a pink fluff of candyfloss on the stick. He turned off the machine, stepped in front of it and handed the stick to Diego, "Strawberry was always your favourite."

"Loco, loco," Diego said, closing his eyes and slapping his forehead. But with his eyes closed the strawberry scent continued to saturate his senses and Diego reopened his eyes and reached for the stick of candyfloss. He sat back on the bench and drew a handful of the fluffy cloud into his mouth. Diego smiled to himself and munched on the candyfloss. His thoughts were filled with a thousand family memories. Eduardo sat beside Diego, and when Diego opened his eyes he told his father his story of the last few weeks.

After Diego had finished his story, he said, "I'm sorry about the money."

"Don't worry, money comes and goes in life."

"Okay. But Papá, I'm all alone now."

"Really? Seems like you've had no problems befriending strangers," Eduardo said, placing a hand on Diego's left shoulder and rising to his feet. "You will never be alone if you are true to yourself."

Eduardo turned to his cart.

"Papá, wait, don't go, I have something for you," Diego said, jumping up.

He ran down the hill and within minutes returned with his father's guitar.

Diego walked up to his father and pushed forward the guitar, "This belongs to you."

"It is yours now. I didn't leave you much, so please keep it, my beautiful boy."

"No, Papá please, it has always been yours. Play something for Mamá."

Diego pushed the guitar forward again.

Eduardo reached for the dark neck of the guitar and said, "You've always been a stubborn one."

"Well, you can't change who you are, can you? And I hope you don't mind but I'm going to keep the case; it will come in handy for the guitar I plan to buy."

With his free arm Eduardo pulled Diego close and Diego embraced his father, hoping the moment would never end. But eventually Eduardo pulled away, gestured to the guitar and raised it to his hip. He turned and headed up the hill.

When Diego could no longer smell the sugary aroma, he glanced over his shoulder. On the ridge of the hill he saw the outline of a figure holding a guitar aloft, almost as if he was serenading someone. Then clouds passed over the moon and Eduardo was gone.

As Diego walked back down the hill he thought of Isa and how stupid he'd been, confusing an angel for a thief. He also thought about Leonardo, and whether he'd reached Santiago yet. And he also wondered if he'd bump into the blonde American again and learn her story. But most of all he thought about the type of guitar he would buy when he reached Santiago.

ENJOYED THIS BOOK?

Reviews are the most important way of spreading the word about my books. And readers, like you, are kindly making a big difference by sharing their views.

So if you enjoyed this book, I would be very grateful if you could spare a few moments more by jumping over to the book's Amazon page and leaving a short honest review too.

By sharing your review, you will be bringing my books to the attention of other readers, which will help me continue to build a loyal readership.

Thank you so much.

Follow Diego's continuing journey in book two of the Reluctant Pilgrim series

Santiago's Guitar

is available at:

Amazon.com

Amazon.co.uk

And all of Amazon's international sites

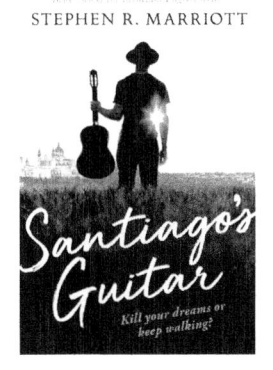

Diego is determined to complete his journey and follow his true path to becoming a flamenco guitarist but he soon discovers that the life of a musician is not an easy one.

Perhaps he still has more roads to walk before he can transform? Journey with Diego along the ancient pilgrim routes as he battles with his demons, meet the people he encounters at their own crossroads and feel the flamenco beating in his heart.

JOIN MY NEWSLETTER

Join Stephen R. Marriott's community to be the first to receive discounts on new book releases, inspiration and other fun things. Most importantly though, building relationships with my readers and the community is the most rewarding thing about being a writer.

There's no spam, your email is safe and I won't bombard you with emails. You can sign up by visiting my website at:

www.stephenrmarriott.com

See you there!

ACKNOWLEDGEMENTS

I'd like to thank my fellow Pilgrims, whom I encountered on the road to Santiago de Compostela in the summer of 2012 and who, along with the whispers in the fields, inspired me to write this novella.

Much love to Eleanor, who had the courage to follow her own course and set me off on my journey and first encouraged me when this story was in its early stages.

Heartfelt thanks to Bill Traugott, who continued to find the time in between his busy life to give me editorial guidance and to translate the stanza from *I Have Walked Down Many Roads*.

My cover designer, Stuart Bache of Books Covered, has created a stunning design for the series.

Last but not least I'd like to acknowledge Lynda Thornhill for her editorial/ proofreading services and Safeena Chaudhry for the book's final touches.

ABOUT THE AUTHOR

Stephen R. Marriott is a British author and traveller. His debut book, *Candyfloss Guitar*, book one of the *Reluctant Pilgrim* series, came about because of his desire to walk a road that millions have walked over the centuries. The people and places that intersected his Camino de Santiago pilgrimage inspired his story of a modern-day pilgrim busking his way across Spain, with little more than his dreams and the gift of his father's old guitar.

Before Stephen broke out of the office and went his own way he worked as an investment analyst for a London stockbroking company. When he's not travelling he normally lays his hat in London.

You can also connect with Stephen at:

: www.facebook.com/StephenRCommunity

: @stephenrmarriott

Email: stephen@stephenrmarriott.com

Printed in Great Britain
by Amazon